In a daring space rescue, three astronauts capture a lost telecommunications satellite. See page 38.
NASA

GET THE MESSAGE

TELECOMMUNICATIONS IN YOUR HIGH-TECH WORLD

by Gloria Skurzynski

BRADBURY PRESS   *New York*
Maxwell Macmillan Canada   Toronto
Maxwell Macmillan International
New York   Oxford   Singapore   Sydney

Your High-Tech World Books
by Gloria Skurzynski
winner of the
American Institute of Physics 1992
Science Writing Award

ROBOTS: Your High-Tech World

ALMOST THE REAL THING:
Simulation in Your High-Tech World

Acknowledgments

To those superb models, Kristin Ferguson and Brian Norton, thank you for bringing this book to life.

Once again, my gratitude to Ed and Lauren, not only for the technical help, but this time for graphics, too. A special thanks to David Nolan. And to Jan.

Bob Ford and Barbara Sweeney at AT&T Bell Labs contributed much to this book—I deeply appreciate their kindness. Bob Alm generously explained concepts and checked pages. For their help, my sincere thanks go to Ron Wiece and Lynn Burt of US West Communications; to Sylvia Kirkwood of GTE; Barbara Kaufman and Timothy Fitzpatrick of Bellcore; Bob Taylor of Conair; Johnny Hales of MobileComm; Mike Paletta of Cellular One; Nancy Levene and Joe Cosgrove of Sharp Electronics; Mike Gentry of NASA; Scott Gardner and Lisa Anderson of Alpha Graphics; David Pinsky of Motorola; to Intelsat; Corning Glass; the Federal Communications Commission; United States Telephone Association; Cellular Telecommunications Industry Association; Bell South; Pacific Bell; and GTE Spacenet.

Thanks also to Bryant Hacking, whose picture appears on page 27, and to Larry Jones, for the use of his 1959 Corvette (page 18). And as always, my appreciation to Barbara Lalicki.

For Tom Andrew Thliveris and
Paul Christopher Thliveris,
both excellent communicators

Bradbury Press
Macmillan Publishing Company
866 Third Avenue
New York, NY 10022

Maxwell Macmillan Canada, Inc.
1200 Eglinton Avenue East
Suite 200
Don Mills, Ontario M3C 3N1

Macmillan Publishing Company is part of the Maxwell Communication Group of Companies.

First edition
Printed and bound in Singapore
10 9 8 7 6 5 4 3 2 1
The text of this book is set in 13 point Sabon.

Library of Congress Cataloging-in-Publication Data

Skurzynski, Gloria.
    Get the message : telecommunications in your high-tech world / by Gloria Skurzynski.—1st ed.
        p.   cm.
    Summary: Explains the scientific principles and technology involved in telephone calls and facsimile transmissions and discusses future possibilities in telecommunications.
    ISBN 0-02-778071-6
    1. Telecommunication—Juvenile literature.   2. High technology—Juvenile literature.   [1. Telephone.   2. Telecommunication. 3. Communication.]   I. Title.
TK5102.4.S58   1993
621.382—dc20   92-14892

CONTENTS

It takes about 7.8 seconds to dial a seven-digit number on a touch-tone phone. A rotary-dial phone takes 3 seconds longer. That doesn't sound like much of a time-saving, but when a central switching office handles 200,000 calls an hour, it makes a difference.

Author photo

WORDS OVER WIRES

Chapter 1

Brian wants to talk to Kristin. He stops at a phone booth outside a convenience store, lifts the receiver off the hook, and drops a quarter into the slot. It all seems so ordinary and so natural that Brian doesn't think much about what he's just done—he's a lot more concerned about what he's going to say.

But Brian has started a complicated procedure. As he puts in the quarter, it triggers a switch. This grounds one of two copper wires running from the pay phone to a nearby telephone pole. From the grounded wire, an electrical current flows to the main computer in the telephone switching office a few miles away. The computer selects a route, through a series of wires that are not being used at that instant, from the switching office back to Brian's pay phone. Over this route, a dial tone buzzes. All this happens in less than a second.

Brian hears the dial tone. With a finger, he pushes the button marked *5*, the first digit in Kristin's seven-digit number. Through the earpiece of the telephone handset, Brian hears a tone—sort of musical, but more electronic than melodious. He pushes *9* and hears a higher tone; pushes *1* and hears a lower tone; and so on, until he's dialed Kristin's number.

Each time Brian pushes a button, an electrical signal goes out over the pair of wires running from the pay phone to the telephone pole nearest him. At the pole, the wire joins a cable that holds 24 other pairs of wires. The cable stretches to a terminal

A repairman's nightmare. In Pratt, Kansas, at the turn of the century, winter blizzards would knock down a lot of telephone wires.
AT&T Bell Labs

on another pole a block away, where it connects with a 200-pair cable. Three blocks farther along the street, the 200-pair cable goes underground and joins an even thicker cable, which holds 2,700 pairs of copper wires. This large cable runs underground all the way to the telephone switching office.

Today, most telephone cables are buried underground. Cables like these can hold from 24 pairs of copper wires to 2,700 pairs.
AT&T Bell Labs

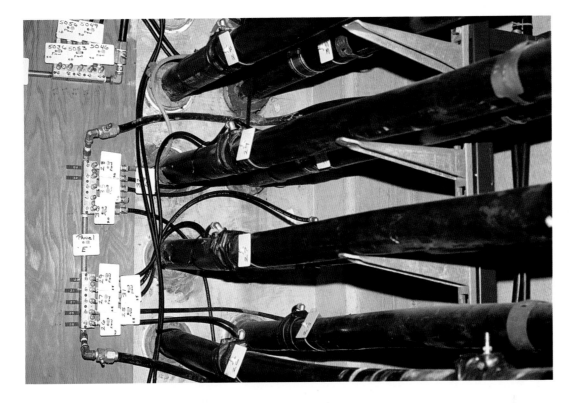

Buried cables emerge from under the city streets into the basement of a telephone company's central switching office.
AT&T Bell Labs

This is not colorful spaghetti; it's just a small portion of the miles and miles of copper wire in a central switching office.

Author photo

Inside the building, a piece of equipment called the tone decoder recognizes each digit Brian has dialed, identifying it by the frequency of its musical tone. Touch-tone dials are faster than rotary dials, the kind where you have to put your finger into holes in a plastic circle and twist. With each digit Brian dials, additional electrical-circuit paths open up in the switching office, one after the other, like dominoes, each pushing over the next one in line. Through sixteen different stages, the master computer decides which paths need to be taken.

Brian's call to Kristin is now at its midpoint. From here, the master computer must locate the two copper wires that run from the switching office all the way to Kristin's house. Those two wires leave the switching office in another one of the big, thick cables, which then divides into smaller and smaller cables until the pair of wires reaches the telephone pole outside Kristin's house. From there, the wires continue into her room.

Before Kristin and Brian can get connected, though, 130 volts of electricity have to travel over the wires to ring the bell in her phone. Brian thinks he hears Kristin's phone ringing, but he really doesn't. What he hears is an electronic signal called a ringback that lets him know his call has gone through. When she picks up her phone, both the actual ringing and the ringback stop.

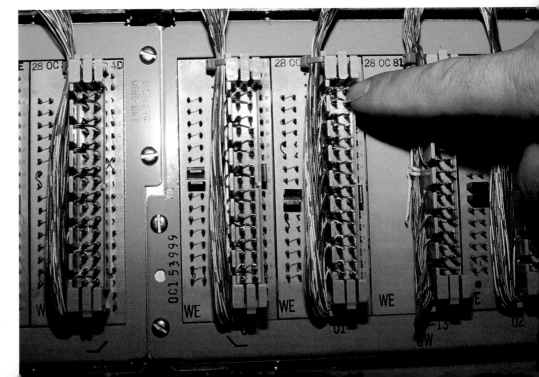

At this point in the central switching office, the pair of copper wires from Brian's phone connects to a pair of copper wires going all the way to Kristin's house, miles away.

Author photo

The plunger in a telephone—in this picture, the deep pink triangle on the left of the phone's base unit—springs up when the receiver is lifted, letting electric current complete a circuit to the central switching office. When the plunger is down, the current shuts off, just the way a light switch on the wall shuts off the lights.

Conair

At that instant, electrical circuits are complete between Brian's phone and Kristin's phone—they're connected. From now on, their conversation takes place over continuous copper wires. Each of them is holding a handset that contains a transmitter and a receiver. *The most important parts of every telecommunications system are the transmitter and the receiver.*

"Hello," Kristin says. Brian knows it's Kristin who has answered the phone, because he recognizes her voice.

"Hi," Brian answers—just that one syllable, but it's enough for Kristin to tell instantly who has called her. Brian sounds like no one else. He has his own, unique voice, and so do you.

In America, callers make more than 400 billion local telephone calls a year. The average business call lasts less than three minutes. The average call on a home phone lasts eight minutes. The average call between teens lasts until a parent shouts, "Are you *still* on that phone?"
Author photo

All sound is caused by vibration. You can watch it happen when someone plucks a guitar string. As the string moves up, it forces the air molecules next to it to move up, too. This squeezes them together and makes an area of high pressure.

When the guitar string bounces back, it pulls apart the molecules behind it, making an area of low pressure. Since the string moves back and forth rapidly, it creates a pattern of high-pressure and low-pressure waves. Sound travels through these waves.

A single vibration—one movement up and one down—is called a cycle. The number of cycles the string vibrates in a second is called its frequency. Remember frequency? It was the frequency of each of those tones on the push buttons that Brian dialed that let the computerized equipment identify the numbers.

Frequency is a way of stating how closely together sound waves are spaced, from the top of one wave to the top of the next. If something vibrates slowly, it has a low frequency; if it vibrates quickly, it has a high frequency. The higher the frequency, the higher the pitch. A high voice has a higher frequency than a low voice.

When you pluck a guitar string (or a rubber band), you create a series of high-pressure and low-pressure waves that cause sound.
From Bionic Parts for People

A person with excellent hearing can hear frequencies from 20 cycles per second to 20,000 cycles per second. Cycles per second are also called hertz. The human speaking voice extends over a range of about 85 hertz to 1,100 hertz—that means all human voices, from those of big, deep-chested men to tiny, squeaky babies. But no single person's speaking voice covers such a wide range. Brian's voice, when he's talking to Kristin, ranges from about 100 to 400 hertz in its basic, or fundamental, range.

Each voice, though, has overtones, or harmonics, which give it its distinctive quality, and these harmonics cover a much wider range—they can go as high as 8,000 hertz. Since the copper wires of a local telephone connection carry only frequencies that range between 300 hertz and 3,500 hertz, some of the high and low harmonic tones in a speaker's voice get cut out. That's why Brian's voice sounds a little different over the telephone than it does when he's talking to Kristin face-to-face. That range, from 300 hertz to 3,500 hertz, is called a bandwidth. *Bandwidth* refers to the difference between the lowest and highest numbers in any frequency range.

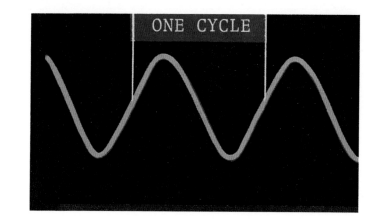

A single vibration—one movement up and down—is called a cycle.
Ed Skurzynski

HUMAN VOICEPRINT

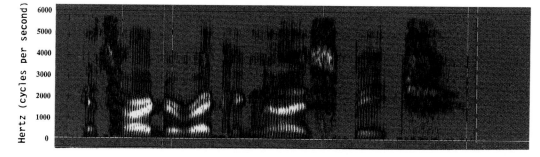

Another name for a voiceprint is a "speech spectrogram." In this picture of the sound waves of a human voice, the bandwidth is measured from bottom to top. Loudness is shown by color.
AT&T Bell Labs

15

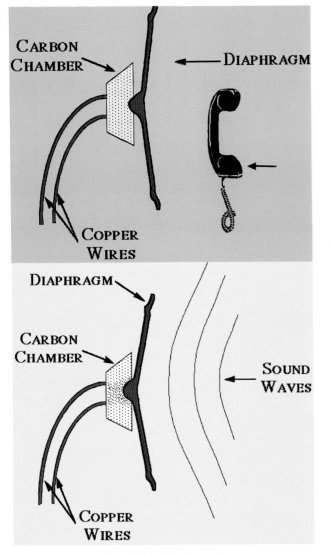

CARBON CHAMBER → **DIAPHRAGM** ←

COPPER WIRES

DIAPHRAGM

CARBON CHAMBER → **SOUND WAVES** ←

COPPER WIRES

TRANSMITTER

Sound waves vibrate the diaphragm in a telephone's transmitter, making grains of carbon squeeze closer together and then pull apart. This increases and decreases the electric current flowing through the wires.

Lauren Thliveris

When Brian says, "Hi," into the mouthpiece of the pay phone, the sound waves from his voice change the strength of the electrical current racing across the wires, increasing and decreasing it. In the phone Brian's using, the mouthpiece—also called a transmitter—has two basic parts: a diaphragm and a carbon chamber. The diaphragm is made of extremely thin metal that vibrates when sound waves hit it, the way a drumhead vibrates when someone beats on it. Lying just underneath the diaphragm, the carbon chamber is filled with tiny grains of charcoal, about the size of grains of sand. These charcoal grains can conduct electricity.

At the "in" position of a sound vibration, the sound waves push the diaphragm against the carbon grains, squeezing them. The tighter they're squeezed, the better they conduct electricity. At the "out" position of a vibration, there's more space between the carbon granules, decreasing the current. This process is repeated hundreds of times a second, as acoustical (sound) energy is converted to electrical energy. The electrical impulses travel over copper wires to Kristin's house in the same frequency patterns as Brian's voice.

Kristin holds the receiver against her ear. Just inside the plastic casing of the phone's earpiece, another diaphragm vibrates. Behind the diaphragm lies an electromagnet—a metal rod with a coil wrapped around it. The increases and decreases of electrical current from Brian's voice affect the electromagnet in Kristin's receiver, pushing *its* diaphragm in and out. This squeezes and then loosens the molecules in the air, creating waves of pressure that exactly match the waves from Brian's voice. In this way, electrical energy is converted back again to acoustical energy.

"Hi, Brian. Where are you?" Kristin asks.

"I'm at the 7-Eleven," he answers.

Since the phone Brian's using and Kristin's phone are located in areas served by the same switching office, theirs is the simplest kind of telephone call that can be made. Brian's voice comes so clearly over the wires that Kristin can almost feel his hesitation.

"I was wondering," he says. "Would you go to the homecoming dance with me?"

Brian can hear Kristin's intake of breath. Even sounds that aren't words create vibrations in air molecules, making waves. In fact, whispers are higher in frequency than spoken words.

"I'd love to go with you," Kristin tells him.

"Okay, fine! See you at school tomorrow." Brian hangs up the phone, breaking the flow of electric current that has carried his voice to Kristin, and hers back to him.

Smiling, Kristin holds the receiver until she hears the dial tone, which tells her that Brian has disconnected. Then she phones her best friend, Andrea. "Guess what!" she says. "Brian just called me."

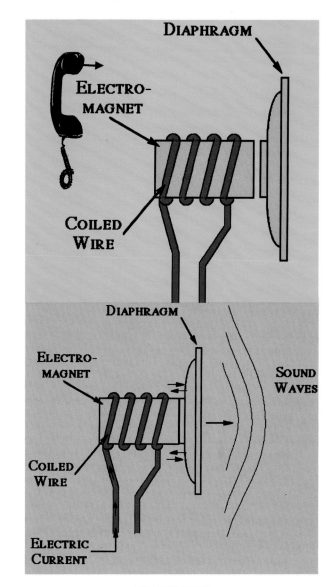

RECEIVER

At the receiving end of a phone call, an electromagnet causes another diaphragm to vibrate, pushing and pulling the air next to it. The vibrations create wave patterns that reproduce sounds.

Lauren Thliveris

Since dialing while driving is unsafe, Brian pulls off the road to make a phone call. "Hands-free" kits can be bought and installed—they let drivers speak aloud to dial the number, then carry on a conversation without holding the handset. "Hands-free" systems work like speaker phones.

Author photo

WORDS ON WAVES *Chapter 2*

Brian is on his way home from his pizza-delivery job. His last delivery was on the outskirts of town. Even though there isn't much traffic on the road, Brian pulls his car to the shoulder and stops before he lifts his mobile phone to dial Kristin's number. Accident reports show that it's impossible to dial, drive, and keep your eyes on the road at the same time.

He pushes the POWER button on the phone. With each digit Brian dials, he sees the number appear on the phone's display panel. After the seventh digit, he pushes the SEND button.

Since Brian is calling from a mobile phone inside his car, there aren't any wires to carry the dialing information to the telephone company's central switching office. Instead, radio waves send the signals to a 200-foot tower a couple of miles away. The tower holds an FM radio receiver that picks up, through an antenna on top, the radio signals coming from Brian's phone.

Radio waves are not the same as the sound waves caused by Brian's vocal cords, or by a vibrating guitar string. Sound waves are pulses of energy caused by air molecules pushing together and pulling apart. Radio waves are created by electromagnetic fields, bursts of electrical energy sent out from one antenna and received by another. Some of the earliest work on radio waves was done a little more than a hundred years ago by a young German scientist named Heinrich Hertz. Recognize the name? His last name became the term for cycles per second.

Radio waves range in frequency from about thirty thousand hertz to three hundred billion hertz. A number that big is hard to imagine, but there's a shorthand you can use when you talk about a lot of hertz. A thousand hertz is called a kilohertz. It's abbreviated kHz. A thousand kilohertz, which is a million hertz, is called a megahertz, abbreviated as MHz. A thousand megahertz, which is a billion hertz, is called a gigahertz, or GHz.

Frequency and power are two very different things. Cellular radio signals are sent at extremely high frequencies and at relatively low power—from 50 to 100 watts. By contrast, a local FM radio station may transmit at a power ranging from 26,000 watts to 100,000 watts.

Each cell tower has a computer, a 50- to 100-watt transmitter, a receiver, and an antenna. The tower picks up radio signals from cellular phones and relays them to a mobile switching office. From there, the calls travel over "landlines."
Cellular One

A cellular-system service territory has a lot of individual radio-coverage areas known as "cells." Cells can range in diameter from one mile to twenty miles, depending on the shape of the land and on the number of people per square mile. As in a honeycomb, the cells connect to one another. Each cell contains a cell site, or tower, with a transmitting antenna and a receiving antenna. If Brian were to keep driving while he used the car phone, a computerized switch would change the frequency as his car moved from one cell site to the next. It would happen so quickly—in one-fifth of a second—that Brian wouldn't even notice it.

A cellular system divides a territory into a honeycomb of cells. As a car drives from one cell to another, the radio frequency of a cellular call changes so fast that the caller doesn't notice it. Adjoining cells can't use the same frequency; cells farther apart can, without getting the signals mixed up.

Graphics by CTIA; color by Scott Gardner and Lisa Anderson

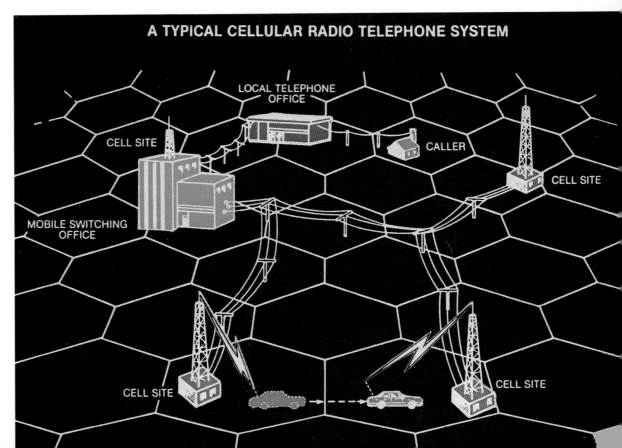

A TYPICAL CELLULAR RADIO TELEPHONE SYSTEM

LOCAL TELEPHONE OFFICE

CELL SITE

CALLER

CELL SITE

MOBILE SWITCHING OFFICE

CELL SITE

CELL SITE

An FM transmitter on the tower relays the signals to a building that houses a mobile switching office. From there they're sent to the same switching office that handled Brian's call to Kristin from the pay phone a few days ago, and from the switching office over wires to Kristin's home. (See diagram on page 21.)

"Hello." Kristin's mother's voice is almost, but not quite, as clear as if it were traveling all the way over copper wires.

"Is Kristin home?" Brian asks.

"She's outside, raking leaves," Kristin's mother says. "Wait a minute—I'll take the cordless phone out to her."

Brian hears a click as Kristin's mother pushes the PHONE button on the cordless phone, transferring Brian's call. The transmitting equipment that sends radio waves to the cordless-phone handset is located in the base unit of the phone. It sends *very* low-power signals that reach only a couple hundred feet from the base unit.

Kristin's mother carries the handset outside. "Hi, Brian," Kristin says.

"How'd you know it was me?"

"My mother told me. Hold on a minute—you sound fuzzy." She pulls out the antenna on the cordless phone as far as it will

Cell towers can be either freestanding or situated on the tops of buildings. People seldom wonder what they're for, or even notice them.
Cellular One

go, making a larger target for the radio signals coming from the base unit inside the house. "That's better. What's up?"

"My boss just told me I have to work the evening of the homecoming dance."

"You mean we can't go?"

"No, we'll still go to the dance—I'm off at seven o'clock. It's just—I wanted to take you to dinner first, but now there won't be time. We can go out to eat afterward, if that's okay with you."

"I didn't hear the last thing you said," Kristin tells him. "There's noise on the line." She turns, changing the direction of the antenna, which helps lessen the static. Cordless phones often pick up interference from other electronic equipment operating in the neighborhood.

"We'll go to Giorgio's after the dance, okay?"

"Perfect! Talk to you later." Kristin pushes the OFF button on the cordless phone. Brian pushes the END button on his car phone.

Because Brian's car stayed parked in the same place, the call was transmitted and received over just one radio channel, or path, out of as many as a hundred channels in a single cell. Each channel has a different frequency, somewhere between 824 and 894 megahertz.

Cordless phones operate on a frequency of 46 to 49 megahertz. The base unit, inside the house, sends out radio signals. Sometimes a call can get crossed with a neighbor's phone conversation.

Author photo

Analog signals are smooth and continuous. Digital signals are divided into chunks. When digital signals carry telephone voices, the sound is clearer. Digital works faster, too.
AT&T Bell Labs

So many people have begun to use cellular phones that the system is running out of radio frequencies. One way to increase the number of calls the system could handle would be to change from analog to digital signals.

The difference between analog and digital signals is like the difference between water pouring from a faucet and ice cubes dropping from an ice maker. An analog signal is a continuously changing voltage. A digital signal is a series of very brief electronic bursts. Digital signals are represented by 1s and 0s, the binary code used by computers (and compact disc players).

Voice sounds (audio waves) usually travel on analog signals carried by radio waves. When the same audio waves are sent by digital signals, the electrical pulses are broken into pieces that can be packed more tightly together, then sorted again into voice

Cellular phones cost anywhere from $200 to $3,000, with the lightweight digital personal communicator phones the most expensive. A digital phone uses less radio bandwidth than an analog phone, allowing the cellular system to handle more calls at the same time.
Motorola

signals at the end of the line. The newest cellular phones transmit digital signals.

Andrea's mother has a digital personal-communicator cellular telephone that weighs just a little more than twelve ounces. As a real estate salesperson, she travels all over the city. If she's in her car, she can use the personal phone there; if she leaves the car, she can carry the same phone in her purse.

It's four-thirty, and she's supposed to pick up Andrea at the gym, but she's not going to make it in time. This happens often enough that she has provided Andrea with a pager—some people call it a "beeper." When Andrea's mother dials the number of her daughter's pager, she hears a signal that tells her to punch in—on the touch-tone buttons of her own phone—the number she wants Andrea to call.

A paging device is a one-way communicator. If you want to respond to a message from a pager, you have to find a phone.
Motorola

At the gym, Andrea is putting things into her gym bag when she hears her pager "beep." The pager's liquid-crystal display window shows the number of her mother's personal phone. Since Andrea's pager is just a signaling device, she can't use it to make a telephone call—she has to go to the pay phone in the hall to dial.

"I'm sorry, honey, I can't pick you up," her mother says. "You'll have to page Dad and tell him to come for you. I don't know when I'll get home—I'm working with a client."

"No problem, Mom," Andrea says. "I'll get in touch with Dad."

Portable telephones, and pagers like this wristwatch model, are already on the job site. Portable fax machines and computers can turn any location into an office.
Motorola

"Grandma, the plane was late, but I'm on my way." From 33,000 feet in the sky, you can reach a telephone anywhere on the ground. Airfones work like any other cellular phones; they send radio signals to ground-station towers that hook up to the public telephone network.
Ed Skurzynski

From the pay phone, Andrea calls the number of her father's pager and punches in the number she's calling from. Andrea's father is a construction engineer; on the job, he wears a wrist-watch pager with an alert-tone signal much louder than a regular beeper, so he can hear it over machinery noises. When he hears the alert signal and sees the number displayed on the face of his watch pager, he walks to his cellular transportable phone—this time he's left it beside the trailer—and dials.

"Dad, can you pick me up at the gym?" Andrea asks when his call reaches her.

"I'm just finishing up here," he tells her. "I'll be there in fifteen minutes."

All these messages—Brian's call to Kristin on her cordless phone, Andrea's mother's signal to her daughter's pager, Andrea's page to her father, his call to her—have taken place through a combination of copper-wire connections and radio signals. But by themselves, radio signals often don't travel far. Not unless they get help.

27

PONY EXPRESS
St. JOSEPH, MISSOURI to CALIFORNIA
in 10 days or less.

☞ WANTED ☜

YOUNG, SKINNY, WIRY FELLOWS
not over eighteen. Must be expert riders, willing to risk death daily.

Orphans preferred.
Wages $25 per week.

APPLY, **PONY EXPRESS STABLES**
St. JOSEPH, MISSOURI

Though the Pony Express lasted only eighteen months before the newly invented telegraph put it out of business, its brave young riders will always be remembered.

In 1860, boys between the ages of fourteen and eighteen spurred their horses to breakneck speeds across prairies and deserts. Every 25 miles or so, each rider would grab the mail pouch his horse carried, hurl the pouch and himself off the weary horse and onto the back of a fresh one, and thunder off toward the next relay station. One hundred and fifty-seven stations, some of them mere shacks in the wilderness, served as relay points along the 1,840-mile Pony Express route.

Today, across those same deserts and across the rest of the United States, microwave towers relay telephone calls, as the Pony Express once relayed pouches of mail. But while the Pony Express took a minimum of eight days to deliver a letter from New York to San Francisco, the microwave relay system delivers a phone call in "real time"—that is, with no delay that the human ear can notice.

Horn antennas catch weakened signals, which are amplified and relayed to the next tower—this happens in a few microseconds. Microwaves with frequencies between one and two gigahertz can carry a thousand times more information than broadcast radio waves with frequencies between one and two megahertz.

AT&T Bell Labs

In your kitchen, several hundred watts of microwave power cook your food. These towers use only twenty watts to transmit microwave signals over a distance of thirty miles.

AT&T Bell Labs

The microwave relay system is incomparably faster than the Pony Express system ever was, but the two share one common practice: replacing a weakened "carrier" with a fresh, strong, energized one.

Tens of thousands of microwave towers crisscross the United States, each of them 25 to 30 miles distant from the next. Since microwave signals travel in a straight line, parallel to the Earth's surface, each tower must be in a direct "line-of-sight" with the next tower in the chain. Any obstacle, like a tall building or a mountain peak, would block the signals.

When a microwave tower transmits a signal—whether the signal is carrying telephone conversations, television programs, or computerized information—it's sent at a power of up to twenty watts. At the end of the first 30-mile stretch, the carrier signal has lost most of its strength, just the way the horses once did. All that's left is about a millionth of a watt.

By then, the weakened signal has reached the next microwave tower in the chain, where a dish-shaped receiver catches it. The millionth-of-a-watt signal travels down a hollow pipe to a shack

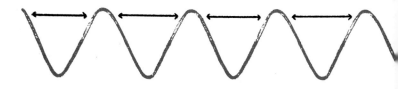

The distance between cycles of a single frequency stays the same no matter how far the waves travel. All electromagnetic waves travel at the speed of light, which is 186,000 miles per second.
Ed Skurzynski

FREQUENCY SPECTRUM

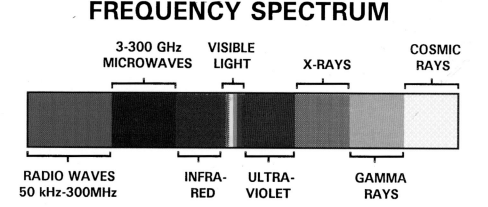

3-300 GHz
MICROWAVES

VISIBLE
LIGHT

X-RAYS

COSMIC
RAYS

RADIO WAVES
50 kHz-300MHz

INFRA-
RED

ULTRA-
VIOLET

GAMMA
RAYS

The higher the frequency, the closer the waves squeeze together. The closer they get, the more signals they can carry.
Ed Skurzynski

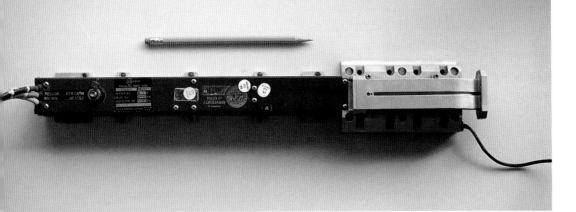

It may not look impressive, but this traveling wave tube can make a weak microwave signal twenty million times stronger.
Wave tube designed by Robert Alm
Author photo

on the ground. There, the very weak signal is built up again to twenty watts. There are two ways to make this happen: by passing the signal through a two-foot-long piece of equipment called a traveling wave tube, or through the solid-state transistors of newer systems.

At full strength once again, the microwave signal is transmitted from another dish-shaped antenna to the next tower some 30 miles away. From one tower to another, all the way across the United States, strong signals get transmitted, lose their strength on the trip, and get caught in the dish-shaped receivers of the next tower in line, where they're strengthened for the next relay. Signals travel this way in 30-mile hops across the continent.

Then they run out of land. The biggest problem with microwave relays is that towers can't be built on oceans. Twenty years ago, if a caller in the United States wanted to phone Madrid, Spain, or Krakow, Poland, the telephone call could travel only as far as the shoreline on microwaves, and then it had to be transferred to thick, wire cables on the ocean floor. Since laying undersea cables was difficult and expensive, there were usually more calls waiting for transmission than there were available paths to carry them. Often, it took hours for a caller to make an overseas connection.

Someone figured out a solution to this problem, but at the time, there was no way to put it into action. In 1945, a young British scientist named Arthur C. Clarke came up with a clever idea. If a space satellite could be launched into orbit, he reasoned, high-frequency radio signals could bounce off the satellite at an angle, the way a billiard ball bounces off the rim of a pool table. If the orbit were high enough—22,340 miles directly above the Earth's equator—the satellite would make a complete circle around the Earth every twenty-four hours—at exactly the same rate that the Earth rotates on its axis. Since both the satellite and Earth would travel at the same speed in relation to each other, the satellite would seem to hover, unmoving, over the same spot on Earth. You can demonstrate this by sticking the tip of a straight pin into an orange. The head of the pin represents a satellite; the orange represents Earth—when you rotate the orange, they move together.

Signals bounced down from a single satellite in this very high orbit could cover one-third of the Earth's surface, Dr. Clarke predicted. Thus, three satellites equally distant from one another could blanket the whole planet with telecommunications signals—except for certain areas close to the North and South Poles, which were mostly unpopulated anyway.

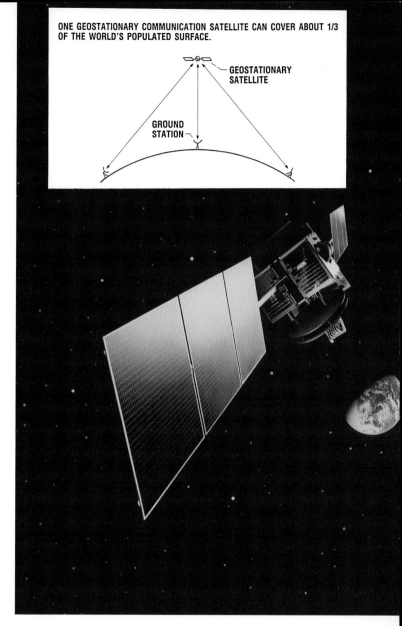

ONE GEOSTATIONARY COMMUNICATION SATELLITE CAN COVER ABOUT 1/3 OF THE WORLD'S POPULATED SURFACE.

GEOSTATIONARY SATELLITE

GROUND STATION

A geostationary satellite stays "parked" above the same spot on Earth. This lets an Earth station's antenna point at the satellite without ever having to change direction.

GTE Spacenet

Arthur C. Clarke was clearly an innovative thinker. In a few years he would write a science-fiction novel called *2001: A Space Odyssey*, which would later become a movie classic. But in 1945, when he first proposed that three satellites in a geostationary orbit could cover the Earth with signals, there wasn't any way to try it out.

Over the next fifteen years, though, lower-orbit satellites were launched successfully. In 1962, AT&T built Telstar I, which a NASA rocket carried into space, making it the first active communications satellite. Telstar was *not* geostationary. As our moon does, it rose and set over the horizon, but at a much faster rate; Telstar I orbited the Earth every 157 minutes. It could transmit six hundred telephone calls at the same time—or one television channel.

The idea of geostationary communications satellites continued to intrigue scientists, and technology was moving ahead at a fast pace. The first telecommunications satellite to "park" in the geostationary orbit—which some scientists were beginning to call "the Clarke Belt"—was Syncom 3, in 1964.

Launched in 1962, Telstar I, shown here, was the first active communications satellite. "Active" means that it could relay signals back to Earth. Three feet in diameter, Telstar I had 72 paneled sides.
AT&T Bell Labs

Many elements have to work together to keep a satellite in a fixed position above the equator. The amount of time it takes a satellite to go around the Earth depends on how high the satellite is. A space shuttle, in an orbit 200 miles high, circles the Earth about every 90 minutes. The Earth-orbiting satellite farthest from our planet—and the one you can actually see—is the moon. At an average distance of 238,857 miles (the distance varies because its orbit is elliptical—that is, closer to Earth at some times than at other times), the moon travels around the Earth once a month, or every 29.53054 days, to be extremely precise.

At about a tenth of the distance between the space shuttle's 90-minute orbit and the moon's 29½-day orbit lies the geostationary orbit, in which each satellite circles the Earth in exactly 24 hours. There are other satellites in other orbits, too, but most communications satellites stay in the same loop, about 22,340 miles up.

Each communications satellite catches weakened signals from Earth. A signal may have started out at a power ranging anywhere from 10 to 3,000 watts. By the time a wave reaches the Clarke Belt, 22,340 miles up, it has weakened to less than a millionth of a watt, or even to a millionth of a millionth of a watt.

Satellites "drift" in space, and are kept within a "control box" by commands from Earth. These people are sending signals that will fire thrusters on a satellite, moving it back where it belongs.
GTE Spacenet

Aboard the satellite, a traveling wave tube or a solid-state power amplifier boosts the signals; devices known as transponders then beam them back down to ground stations. Some of the ground-station antennas are huge; others can be as small as your neighbor's TV satellite dish, which doesn't have to be large, because it only receives signals and doesn't transmit them.

More than two hundred communications satellite *systems* are parked in the geostationary orbit right now. The largest system, Intelsat, has seventeen satellites in orbit. Arthur C. Clarke's idea that only three satellites could blanket the Earth with signals was correct, but three satellites couldn't begin to handle today's volume of phone calls, television programs, and business information. That's even though today's advanced communications satellites, the ones that use the most complex, signal-squeezing, signal-multiplying digital technology, can carry up to 120,000 telephone calls *and* three color television channels at the same time. Compare that to what Telstar could do in 1962!

Many communications satellites are launched from the jungles of French Guiana aboard Ariane rockets. The cost of putting a satellite into geostationary orbit can reach hundreds of millions of dollars.
GTE Spacenet

Like a giant hand cupped to catch signals from space, an Earth-station reflector dish looms above Indonesian boys playing soccer. Earth-to-satellite signals range from 10 to 3,000 watts when they start out. Moving through Earth's atmosphere weakens them.

Intelsat

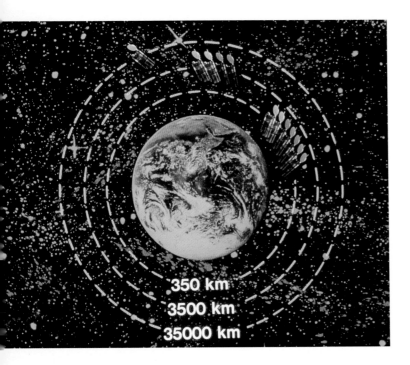

350 km
3500 km
35000 km

American space shuttles travel in LEOs—low-Earth orbits—about 350 kilometers (217 miles) above Earth. The geostationary orbit is at an altitude of 22,340 miles (35,952 kilometers.) Few satellites use the space in between.
AT&T Bell Labs

Sometimes a mishap lands a satellite in the wrong place. In 1990, a failed launch attempt left the four-and-a-half ton Intelsat VI F-3 in a useless low orbit. Two years later, in May 1992, crew members of the brand-new space shuttle *Endeavor* rendezvoused with the stranded Intelsat VI. As millions of television viewers watched during three tension-filled days, astronaut Pierre Thuot struggled to attach a bar to the revolving communications satellite. Because everything is weightless in space, Thuot's slightest touch caused the satellite to wobble and move away.

As a last resort, astronauts Rick Hieb and Tom Akers joined Thuot outside the *Endeavor* to grab hold of the Intelsat in their gloved hands. They lowered it to the shuttle's cargo bay, where they attached a reboost motor and then sent the satellite back into space. Hours later it was boosted into a proper geostationary orbit.

After its capture, a reboost rocket was attached to the bottom of Intelsat VI. When fired, the rocket sent the satellite into the correct orbit.

NASA

"I have a problem," Kristin tells her best friend, Andrea. "Last night my grandmother called, and my mom told her about this picture from the homecoming dance. So now she wants to see it."

"What's the problem?" Andrea asks.

"I only have one copy of the picture, and my grandmother lives two thousand miles away! If I mail this to her, and then she mails it back, it might get wrinkled or lost or something."

"Fax it," Andrea suggests. "You can fax color pictures if you have a color fax machine, and my dad has one at his office. They use it to send architectural drawings and stuff like that. I bet if you asked him, my dad would take your picture to work and fax it to your grandmother. Only, your grandmother would need a color fax machine, too, on that end, to receive the picture."

"She might have one where she works," Kristin says. "It's a big advertising agency. I'll call her tonight and find out."

Author photo

Sharp Electronics Corporation, of Mahwah, New Jersey, has manufactured the first full-color desktop facsimile/copier. Moving from top to bottom, it scans very thin lines on a picture, and assigns a code to each dot of color. It then transmits the codes over telephone wires.

Sharp Electronics Corporation

The next morning, Andrea's father takes the picture of Kristin and Brian to the office of his construction engineering company. At 10:33, the machine on his desk starts to scan the photograph. Three minutes later and two thousand miles away, Kristin's grandmother holds a perfect reproduction of the homecoming photo. The original photograph is still on Andrea's father's desk; he'll return it to Kristin that evening.

When Andrea's father faxed the photograph, 1,728 sensors in a single computer chip sampled tiny dots of color—four hundred dots in every linear inch of the photograph. Each dot was analyzed to determine which combination of red, green, and blue would produce that color. As the sensors moved down the photograph, they gave each dot a code number based on the dot's color combination. The numbers were then transmitted over telephone lines in bursts of digital information, using the 1s and 0s of binary code. At the other end of the transmission, the fax machine in Kristin's grandmother's office began to print out the picture.

In the fax machine, the colors get printed one at a time—first yellow, then blue, then red—on mylar-coated paper. By the third and final printing, the three colors have blended into a full-color reproduction. The finished fax is so faithful to the original that it's hard to tell the two apart.

Black-and-white fax machines have been around for a long time. The first facsimile system ("fax" is short for facsimile) was invented in Scotland 150 years ago. It was used to transmit news photos.

Color fax machines didn't appear in the United States until the end of 1991. At a price of thirty-two thousand dollars for one machine—and remember, two are needed: one for sending and one for receiving—they haven't yet reached a lot of customers. But new technology usually starts out high-priced, and then gets less expensive as scientists and engineers discover better and cheaper ways to manufacture the products.

Although expensive paper and ribbon raise the cost of a color fax to three dollars per page, the copy looks as clear and true as the original photo.
Ed Skurzynski; color fax by Sharp Electronics Corporation

Strands of flexible glass fiber as thin as a human hair carry telephone conversations on laser pulses.
AT&T/Insight

Perhaps you noticed that the three colors that are *transmitted*—red, green, and blue—are different from the three colors the receiving machine *prints*—red, yellow, and blue. In *light* transmissions, red, green, and blue combine to produce all the colors of the rainbow. An example is the three-color picture tube in your television set. In *printing*, the primary colors are yellow, red, and blue, the pigments you've been mixing together in poster paints since you were in kindergarten. They, too, combine to make every possible shade that can be painted or printed—sixteen million in all.

Faxes, whether they're in color or black-and-white, are sent over telephone lines. The quality of the finished copy depends on the quality of the telephone transmission. The fax Kristin's grandmother received looked especially fine, because the signals had traveled mostly over *fiber-optic cable*.

In the past few years, thousands of miles of copper wire in telephone networks have been replaced by strands of glass, each one as thin as a human hair. The glass is so pure that if the oceans were made of it, you could look down and see every sunken ship in the deepest trenches on the ocean floor.

This new system, which sends information over glass fibers rather than copper wires, is called the "lightwave" system. Instead of electricity, it uses a stream of laser light to carry signals over the glass fibers, which are also called optical fibers, or fiber optics.

The word "laser" is an acronym—it comes from the first letters of the phrase "*Light Amplification by Stimulated Emission of Radiation*." The term describes how lasers operate: When atoms are "stimulated" by a voltage, they give up excess electrons, which create a very pure light beam.

The second word in the term should probably have been "oscillation" rather than "amplification," says laser physicist Robert Bertolini. However, he adds, "The old joke goes that, if you called it an oscillator, the acronym would come out *LOSER* rather than *LASER*. And . . . who would ever work on a project called 'loser'?"

Laser beams are directional, which means they don't spread out the way other light does. They can be aimed over long distances and still remain tightly focused.
AT&T Bell Labs

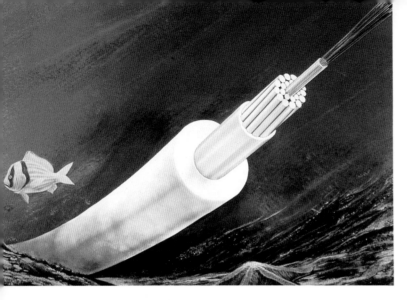

Sharks like to bite cables on the ocean floor. That's why a narrow bundle of optical fibers is covered with layers of protective material.
AT&T Bell Labs

In a lightwave system, electrical signals are converted to a billion flashes per second of laser light carrying a coded pattern of 1s and 0s. Just the opposite happens at the receiving end, where a photo detector transforms the flashes back to electrical signals.

Lasers are different from ordinary visible light. Light from a light bulb scatters every which way. Laser light flies straight as an arrow, in a very narrow beam, hardly spreading at all. But like all electromagnetic waves, lasers can travel only so far before they grow weak. (Remember how the weak microwave signals had to be strengthened by a traveling wave tube, or by transistors, before they could be relayed?) Lasers traveling through glass fibers are strengthened by devices called optical amplifiers. The newest kind can boost signals in midpath without having to convert them from lightwave to electronic and back again.

In recent experiments, lightwave signals of specially shaped optical pulses called solitons were sent six thousand miles *without* being strengthened—far enough to cross the Pacific. Fiber-optic cables work better under oceans than copper cables do. They're narrower and stronger, and they don't suffer as much damage when sharks gnaw on them.

The crew on AT&T's cable ship *Long Lines* lowers an undersea lightwave cable. The orange buoys keep the cable afloat until a sea plow can bury it. Today, transoceanic cables carry 40,000 conversations at once. In the future, they'll carry 600,000.
AT&T Bell Labs

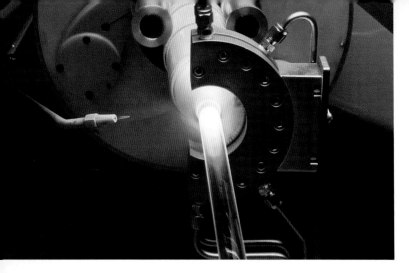

A torch heats a glass tube in a research lab. After chemicals are added, the glass is drawn into optical fibers.
Bellcore

At this time, optical fiber is more expensive to make than copper wire, but the cost will eventually come down. After all, optical fiber is made from one of the most common minerals on Earth: silicon dioxide, the main ingredient in sand. But optical fiber has to be made exceptionally pure, and remain that way, to work properly. This is how it's done:

High above a factory floor, a glass rod as thick as a broomstick glows inside a 2,000-degree-Centigrade furnace. From the white-hot tip of the rod, several miles of clear glass will be drawn out, the way a thin string of cheese stretches from the top of a hot pizza when you lift a slice. As the hair-fine glass is drawn, it's coated with thin, yellowish plastic for protection against dust and weather. At the rate of seventeen feet per second, it gets coiled around a spool, which is then stacked on a shelf with hundreds of other spools waiting for shipment.

To visualize an optical fiber, think of a thermometer with a column of red mercury inside. Now imagine the thermometer stretched until it's as thin as a human hair, and imagine that the narrow core that once held mercury is instead a tunnel for laser light. One more thing—imagine that this hair-thin glass can bend in a full circle without breaking, and when it's looped into circles, the light inside bends with it.

An optical fiber is 125 micrometers in diameter. The core inside the fiber—the narrow tunnel through which the laser travels—is only 8 micrometers in diameter. There are 25,400 micrometers in an inch. You can see why, even when hundreds of these glass fibers are bundled together to make a cable, it will be much narrower than a copper-wire cable.

Spools wound full of optical fiber are stored before being shipped from the factory in Atlanta, Georgia. One single strand of fiber is capable of carrying every phone conversation in New York City on an especially busy day.

AT&T Bell Labs

Fiber-optic transmission works faster, since optical fibers have higher transmission capacity, or bandwidth. That's because lasers operate in the lightwave segment of the electromagnetic spectrum, the part that has infrared, visible-light, and ultraviolet waves (see page 31). In that segment, the frequencies (cycles per second) range from one hundred trillion hertz to ten quadrillion hertz. (Ten quadrillion is written as a one with sixteen zeros after it.) All electromagnetic waves travel at the same speed—the speed of light—but the higher a wave's frequency, the more information it can carry. And the bigger the load the wave carries, the faster an entire information package can get where it's going.

Example: If you wanted to move ten tons of coal from London to Newcastle, and you used a wagon that could haul one ton at a time, you'd get the whole load there faster than if you carried it bushel by bushel. To bring that example up to the twenty-first century, supremely high-frequency waves packed with information can transfer information faster than lower-frequency waves, which can't carry as much at a time. For instance, in just one second, using optical fiber, you could transmit a one-and-a-half-hour television program. Or all the words in sixteen Bibles.

Since optical fibers are so thin, splicing them—joining two ends together—takes steady hands and a jeweler's magnifying glass. If the ends don't meet properly, voice signals get garbled. Imagine doing this job thirty feet above a busy highway!
AT&T Bell Labs

Even though, in theory, it's possible to send that much information quickly, in practice, it rarely happens. "In theory" means what is possible; "in practice" means what usually takes place. Often, equipment is capable of performing more than the world needs at a particular time. But once a new technology catches on, the world manages to catch up, often sooner than expected. And fiber optics are catching on everywhere, not just under oceans, but aboveground and below ground, crisscrossing a number of nations like lace. Almost five million miles of fiber-optic cable have been laid across the United States alone.

In certain large cities, so many thick, copper-wire cables were installed underground that the cities' manholes and utility tunnels began to get clogged. Since fiber-optic cable takes up less space, many cities are removing the old, thick, copper cables and replacing them with fiber-optic cables.

Fiber-optic technology keeps improving. Not long from now, a fiber-optic cable half an inch thick will be able to transmit and receive two and a half million telephone conversations at the same time.

But telephone conversations aren't the only things fiber optics will carry.

Scientists continually work to improve lightwave systems. A new technique will switch and process light signals in trillionths of a second.
Bellcore

AT&T's VideoPhone 2500 has a liquid-crystal display screen and a camera lens (the little circle above the screen). The unit plugs into an ordinary telephone outlet.

AT&T Bell Labs

Question: What do you do if you're just getting out of the shower and your hair is dripping wet, and the telephone rings? **Answer:** You grab a towel and answer the phone. But first, close the shutter over the camera lens so the person on the other end of the call won't see how soggy you look.

In 1992, AT&T introduced the world's first full-color, motion videophone. The AT&T VideoPhone 2500 transmits and receives video calls over ordinary home-telephone lines for the same price as for voice calls alone. No fancy installation is necessary—you just take it home, plug it in, and make a call. If the person you call has a videophone, too, you can have a face-to-face conversation across the miles.

"A whole generation of young people is demanding video technology," says AT&T's Kenneth Bertaccini. "I believe that by the year 2001, visual communications will become as important to consumers as wireless communications."

In Bellcore's Cruiser system, color cameras and monitors are linked from desktop to desktop. This lets people see, and not just hear, how others react to a new idea.
Bellcore

If you can't afford fifteen hundred dollars to buy a videophone, you can rent one for thirty dollars a day. If you don't want to rent one, you can use a pay videophone in a hotel lobby or at an airport. And if you'd like to check out how you're going to look to the person you're calling, you can touch a button that will put your own image on the screen in front of you. Hair okay? Sweater straight? Press the button, and your image is transmitted across the wires, looking terrific.

A videophone isn't the only product that lets you see the person on the other end of the line. In a few homes today, people can carry on phone conversations while they watch each other on their own television screens. But VideoPhone 2500 is available right now, while the other system is still being developed. GTE, a major communications corporation, is conducting a high-tech experiment in Cerritos, California, a medium-size city twenty-five miles southeast of Los Angeles.

In Cerritos, hundreds of homes are wired in one of three ways: with ordinary, copper cables; with coaxial cables (the kind used by most cable television systems); or with fiber optics. Of the three, the system with almost unlimited capacity is fiber optics. Telephone, television, audio, and computer information can be integrated over fiber optics in a way that was never possible before.

All the information is carried in digital form. As you remember, the binary code uses 1s and 0s to send digital information. Each 1 or 0 is called a bit; it's the smallest unit of information recognized by a computer. The word "bit" is a contraction of "binary digit." Several bits make up a byte, or a computer word. A fiber-optic channel can carry at least two million bits of information per second—that classifies it as a "broadband" system. Copper wires can't handle a wide enough bandwidth to bring video, audio, voice, computer, and fax transmissions into your house all over the same wires. Fiber optics can.

Fiber-optic cable is fed down a manhole into an underground telecommunications network. It will connect several homes in Cerritos, California.
GTE

Talk to a friend over TV. This system uses your own camcorder, your own television set, and your own telephone to give you a full-motion video of the person you're calling. Also needed: a fiber-optic hookup to both houses.
GTE

If you lived in one of the houses in Cerritos with a fiber-optic hookup, you could:

Take a class over television, interacting with the teacher. Suppose you want to learn Chinese, but your school doesn't offer classes in Chinese. With an *integrated services digital network* in your home (it's easier to say "ISDN", or just "fiber-optic hookup") you can be in a class by yourself. You and the teacher will look at each other by way of video camcorders, each seeing the other's image on your television screens. When you make a mistake in pronunciation or grammar, he corrects you. When you write a Chinese word, you can hold up the paper to the camcorder, and he'll see whether you've written it correctly.

There's more. If you wake up sick, and your mother doesn't want to leave you alone, she can "telecommute"—stay home, but connect to her job through her computer and video terminals. Suppose you break out in spots; your mother calls the doctor, who examines you through the two-way video hookup. It's not chicken pox, the doctor tells you, peering closely at the screen in her office. Looks more like a rash from some food you're allergic to; probably the same food that upset your stomach.

You get bored just lying around covered with spots, and your mother is still working on her computer, so you phone the film library to order a movie—you choose one from hundreds of titles. It instantly appears on your television screen. You fast-forward over the dumb parts, then put it on pause when your friend calls to ask why you weren't in school. While you're on the phone, your mother checks her bank balance on the TV screen, then calls up a clothing-catalog display to order a new pair of jeans for you.

From the video-on-demand library in Cerritos, a selected videotape will be transmitted directly to a customer's TV set. It's like renting a tape without having to pick it up or take it back.
GTE

The TV screen connects these students to other classrooms and to outstanding learning experiences. It's all live-action, which means they can interact in real time—ask questions, show pictures, and share information about projects.
GTE

All these communications have come into your house over the same thin strands of optical fiber. Most people won't have this technology in their homes for twenty years, but in Cerritos, it's happening now. This experiment will help determine what people want and need in the homes of the future.

Some planners are wondering if all this is really necessary. Linking every home in the United States with fiber optics could cost at least $230 billion, and would take decades to complete. Would it be worth it? What do you think? (By comparison, the Pentagon asked for $278.3 billion for defense spending for one year—1992.)

Certainly, businesses, hospitals, and schools can benefit a great deal from digitized fiber-optic communications. Imagine this scene:

Your spots have gone away, so you go back to school. After lunch, your class and another class in a school across town have a spelling contest, via video conferencing—you watch each other on your TV screens as your class spells down the other side. Next, all the classrooms in town see and hear a talk by a biologist who has grown a new high-yield rice that will help feed the world. She's in her lab showing you her experiments. You're in your classroom, but, by video hookup, you ask her questions and she answers them. It's a wonderful learning experience.

The Japanese are planning to have fiber optics in every home in their nation by the year 2015. Whether or not that happens in the United States, our technical know-how will keep racing ahead. In the twenty-first century, our telephone, television, and computer systems will be linked to make one vast, powerful, user-friendly network. Researchers are already working on it.

Scientists and engineers find real excitement in discovering new concepts and developing new technologies. Every day, they're eager to get to their jobs, eager to talk with other scientists and other "techies" about what they're doing. What makes their work even more exciting is that they can't always predict how things will turn out.

Theoretical physicist Shirley Jackson says, "In physics, when you finally do see what you're looking for . . . someone can go into the lab and hopefully make a structure that behaves in the way you predicted. What you found could one day advance communications technology . . . [perhaps] open up new uses for fiber optics."

Or new methods of "wireless" communications: the personal digital phones and pagers that keep growing lighter and smaller.

Theoretical physicist Shirley Jackson says about scientific intuition, "It's a feeling of being pulled in a certain direction. You just 'know' something is leading you to something that's never been observed before. You'll be the first to see it."
AT&T Bell Labs

The ultimate goal may be to provide a personal phone number to everyone, something like a social security number, that will allow people to be reached wherever they are. Says Bob Lucky of AT&T Bell Labs, "In the future, we'll all have Dick Tracy telephones on our wrists, and never be out of touch. Unless we choose to be."

People the world over will reach out to touch one another's lives.

Speak kindly. And listen well.

**Wouldn't you be eager to get to the lab
if you had state-of-the-art tools like this
to work with?**
AT&T Bell Labs

Glossary

analog continuous and uninterrupted, as in the circling motion of the hour hand of a clock

antenna a wire, rod, or similar device that sends or receives electromagnetic waves and converts them to electrical signals

AT&T American Telephone and Telegraph, the major telephone network in the United States

bandwidth the information-carrying capacity of a communications channel, measured in bits per second or cycles per second

binary the base 2 number system that uses only 1s and 0s to express all numbers

bit the smallest unit of information in a computer: represented in binary as a 1 or 0

byte a unit made up of eight bits

carbon chamber a cup holding granules of carbon; when sound waves push the granules closer together, electric current passes through them more easily

carrier a radio-frequency signal that is modulated (altered by amplitude, frequency, or phase) to carry information

cellular land-mobile communications system; a city or county is divided into cells, each with a low-powered radio transmitter/receiver for relaying calls

channel a specific frequency used to transmit information electronically

circuit a path for transmitting electric current

conduct to transfer electricity over wire

control box the area a satellite must remain inside to be geostationary

current the flow of electrons through a conductor

cycle a wave consisting of one peak and one trough

diaphragm a circular piece of thin metal that vibrates in a telephone transmitter or receiver

digital discrete (distinct, divided, interrupted), in contrast to the continuity of analog signals or functions

digital modulation alteration of a carrier frequency into two distinct states representing 1 and 0

downlink transmission path from a satellite to an Earth station

electromagnet a metal core surrounded by a wire coil; when current flows through the wire, the core becomes magnetic

electromagnetic spectrum the entire range of frequencies from lowest (radio waves) to highest (gamma waves, cosmic waves)

fax short for facsimile; the transmission of an image by electrical or light signals over telephone lines

fiber optics hair-thin, hollow strands of pure glass through which information encoded as pulses of light is transmitted

FM (frequency modulation) varying the frequency of a carrier wave in accordance with the sound being transmitted

frequency the number of times per second that a cycle is repeated

geostationary a circular satellite orbit 22,300 miles above the equator; the orbital period is 24 hours

GHz gigahertz; one billion cycles per second

ground electrical connection with the ground; the ground is electrically neutral

handset a telephone mouthpiece and receiver mounted in a single unit

harmonic tone an overtone whose rate of vibration is a multiple of a fundamental tone

hertz cycles per second

interference static or other unwanted signals that degrade or distort a signal source

ISDN Integrated Services Digital Network; a system that lets voice, data, and image signals travel together over the same optical fibers

kHz kilohertz; a thousand cycles per second

laser a very intense, narrow beam of light formed by light waves that have been amplified and concentrated

LEO low-Earth orbit

lightwave a system that uses pulses of laser light to transmit billions of bits of information per second through optical fiber

liquid crystal a fluid solution that can be activated electrically to form numbers or letters, as on a digital watch

MHz megahertz; a million cycles per second

micrometer one micron; one millionth of a meter

microwaves high-frequency radio waves, with frequencies ranging from one gigahertz to one terahertz; microwaves travel in line of sight

mobile phone the type of cellular phone that is installed in a car or a truck; it is powered by the vehicle's battery

modulation the process of encoding a signal on a carrier wave by varying its frequency, amplitude, or phase

optical amplifier a device to boost weak fiber-optic signals

pitch in music or speech, the location of a tone on the scale

power the amount of electrical energy delivered to a circuit, expressed in watts

pulse a brief surge of electrical energy

radio waves electromagnetic waves with frequencies ranging between ten kilohertz and one gigahertz

receiver equipment for converting electronic signals or electromagnetic waves back to audible sound

static electrical discharges that interfere with reception

switching office the central building where incoming telephone calls are connected to outgoing lines

terahertz one trillion cycles per second

transistor a solid-state device that amplifies, controls, or generates electrical signals

transmitter equipment for converting sound signals to electronic signals or radio waves

transponder the electronic equipment on a satellite that amplifies and then retransmits a signal received from Earth

uplink transmission path from an Earth station to a satellite

volt unit of electric force

watt unit of electric power

Index